Georgie

Georgie tingled all over. She'd never ever danced on a real stage before, and her body was bursting with excitement as she began the routine...

ORCHARD BOOKS
96 Leonard Street, London EC2A 4XD
Orchard Books Australia
Unit 31/56 O'Riordan Street, Alexandria, NSW 2015
First published in Great Britain in 2002
A PAPERBACK ORIGINAL
Text © Ann Bryant 2002
Series conceived and created by Ann Bryant
Series consultant Anne Finnis
The right of Ann Bryant to be identified as the author
of this work has been asserted by her in accordance with the
Copyright, Designs and Patents Act, 1988.
A CIP catalogue record for this book is available
from the British Library.
ISBN 1 84121 784 0
1 3 5 7 9 10 8 6 4 2
Printed in Great Britain

Make Friends With
Georgie

Ann Bryant

ORCHARD BOOKS

Chapter One

It was the middle of the school holidays. Georgie and her mum were going into town. While her mum walked, Georgie did a dance routine that she'd made up.

"Don't get too far ahead now," called her mum.

But Georgie didn't hear her because she'd just thought of a rap to go with the routine. She was saying it loudly as she jogged and clapped and clicked and kicked...

"Well we're goin' into town,

Yeah we're goin' into town.

With a tip and a tap and a rippa rippa rap.

First we're goin' to the library,

Then we're goin' to the shops.

With a tip and a tap and a rippa rippa rap.

Then we're goin' back home for a great big lunch,

With a chip chip chip and a choc chip crunch.

YEAH!"

As Georgie danced and rapped her way along the street she passed quite a few people. They all smiled at her. And Georgie smiled right back.

She'd got all the way to the Playhouse Theatre before she stopped and turned round. Uh-oh! Her mum was very far behind – just a tiny little dot in the distance. Georgie had gone a bit further than she'd meant to. She thought she'd better make her way back before her mum started to get cross. She got ready for a fast sprint. *On your marks…get set…*

But Georgie stayed rooted to the spot because she heard a voice. There was no one in front of her and no one behind her. She looked across the road. She looked all round again. Nothing. So she just stayed very still and listened hard.

There it was again. A man was calling something out. His voice seemed to be coming from inside the theatre. Halfway along there was a door that wasn't quite shut. Georgie really *really* wanted to go inside and investigate, but she knew her mum would tell her off for going into a strange place. She looked down the road. Her mum was still very far away. There would be enough time to nip inside, have a look and nip back out again without her mum even knowing.

She opened the door carefully, crept inside and found herself standing in a long dark passage. Now she could hear the man's voice clearly, but she didn't understand what on earth he was saying.

"...*Be as thou wast wont to be... See as thou wast wont to see...*"

He must come from another country, thought Georgie. She liked the sound of the strange words so much that she couldn't help herself tiptoeing along the corridor towards the voice. But then a woman started talking in the same funny language.

"...*Methought I was enamoured of an ass...*"

Georgie had turned a corner into a shorter passage. This one was even darker. On a high shelf was an enormous pretend donkey's head and on the floor were boxes full of material flowers. At the end, standing next to a sort of huge screen, were two men and a lady. They had their backs to Georgie and were watching the people who were talking.

Georgie's eyes widened and a burst of excitement swirled around her body. She suddenly realised that she was standing at the side of a real stage. And the people were proper actors and actresses, practising their play. She couldn't help a little gasp escaping. Then she clapped her hand to her mouth because one of the men swung round sharply. The look he gave her was so fierce that all the strength went out of Georgie's legs.

★ ★ ★

Chapter Two

Half of Georgie wanted to run away because the scary man was coming towards her and she knew all about not talking to strangers. But the other half wanted to stay right there and listen to the actors on the stage.

"Can I help you?" the man asked in a hushed voice. But Georgie was too excited to speak so she just looked at him with round brown eyes. "Are you looking for someone?" he tried again.

"I heard the acting and I wanted to see," said Georgie in a croaky whisper.

The man frowned and bent right down so his ear was beside Georgie's mouth. "What's that you say?"

"I wanted to see the acting."

When the man straightened up again he was smiling.

"And have you come on your own?"

"My mum's outside."

"We don't usually let people watch rehearsals." Georgie's face fell. "But if it's just you and your mum, I suppose that would be all right."

"Brilliant!" said Georgie, doing a little bounce, now the strength was back in her legs.

"Ssh!" said the man, putting his finger to his lips. "You have to be completely quiet if you stay here in the wings."

Georgie nodded hard. Her eyes were bigger than ever and her lips were tight shut, to show the man how quiet she could be. But somehow, she had to let him know that she was just going to tell her mum where she was. She pointed to herself, pointed to the door, pointed to her watch, put one finger up, and hoped that the man understood her.

He grinned and whispered, "Great mime! You're just going to tell your mum, and you'll be back in one minute... Yes?"

Georgie nodded even harder, then jogged away with her lightest footsteps.

After the dark corridor, it seemed as though someone had switched a bright light on to the street outside. Georgie looked to right and left but her mum was nowhere in sight.

She must have gone a bit ahead, thought Georgie, so she set off running towards the town. There was a tiny drop of worry inside her tummy because she'd never been all on her own like this before.

The more she ran, the bigger the drop grew. And by the time she came to the turn-off to the library, the drop had spread right round the inside of her body.

That's funny, I'm sure Mum couldn't have got this far already, she said to herself. She would have waited for me.

Georgie stood there wondering which way to go – towards the library or towards the High Street where the shops were. She hardly ever cried, but at that moment she could feel tears pricking the backs of her eyes. She tried to think what her mum would tell her to do. But all she could think of was phoning, and she didn't know where the phone box was.

Then right out of the blue she had a bit of a scary idea. She would run back to the theatre and ask that nice actor if he'd got a mobile phone so she could phone her mum's mobile number and find out where she was! Her mum would be pleased with her then, for being so sensible and grown-up. Brilliant!

Chapter Three

Georgie ran all the way back to the door that led to the stage. Then she crept inside and tiptoed down the dark passage and round the corner. The man was still standing there at the side of the stage. And on the stage were lots of people. They seemed to be having some kind of argument. Not a real one of course — just part of their play. She tapped the man gently on his back and he jumped as though a wasp had stung him.

When he realised the wasp was Georgie, he started looking round.

"Where's your mum?" he whispered.

"I've lost her."

"You've *what*!"

"I've lost her. But don't worry, I can phone her mobile number."

The man looked at her as though she'd turned into a pink gorilla. "You don't seem very worried for a kid who's lost her mum!"

"I was nearly crying a few minutes ago," Georgie told him. "But I'm all right now I've thought of the mobile."

The man grinned. "My name's Mitch, by the way."

"Mine's Georgie... So, er, have you got a phone I can borrow, please?"

"Er...no... Not on me." He was patting his pockets and frowning.

"Someone's sure to have one, but they're all busy at the moment. We mustn't interrupt them when they're in the middle of a scene. You'll have to wait a few minutes."

But Georgie knew what her mum was like. She could get very cross in a very short time.

"The trouble is, my mum will be worried about me," she whispered.

Mitch looked as though he wasn't sure what to do. Then he took a couple of steps forwards, and hissed at the nearest person on the stage.

"Emma, got your mobile on you?" A lady with long blonde hair turned round looking very annoyed. "Sorry," Mitch went on. "Kid's lost her mum." He shrugged with his palms turned up as though it wasn't *his* fault.

Emma pulled the phone off her belt and handed it to Mitch without saying a word. Then she turned back to the play.

"Thanks," said Georgie.

Mitch switched it on. "There. Now, keep your voice down, all right?"

Georgie nodded and tapped in the number. Her mum answered straight away.

"Hi Mum, it's me."

"Where are you? I've been worried sick!"

Georgie took a few steps away from the stage so she could talk in a normal voice and not disturb the actors.

"Sorry, Mum. I heard a voice and went in to see who was talking. They're rehearsing a play in the theatre."

"Georgie? Georgie? Are you there?"

"Can't you hear me, Mum?"

"Georgie…?"

"I'm in the Playhouse!"

"Keep it quiet," said Mitch, flapping his hand, and looking very worried.

And that was when Georgie suddenly realised she'd been shouting. She felt her face go hot as her eyes travelled past Mitch, to the people on the stage. They were all standing still. All staring. No one was speaking. One or two of them were even glaring at her.

★ ★ ★

Chapter Four

Georgie suddenly realised she'd done a terrible thing. She'd made everyone stop right in the middle of the rehearsal, because of her loud voice. She felt ashamed of herself.

"Can we *please* get on?" said Emma, looking furious.

"She's only a kid," said Mitch. "She's lost her mum and the signal for the mobile's no good in this theatre. No wonder she was speaking a bit loudly."

"A *bit*! Huh!" said Emma.

"Try out there," someone else said, pointing to the back of all the empty seats in the auditorium.

"Go down these steps at the side of the stage here," said Mitch. But he was too late. Georgie had already gone on to the stage and bounded lightly off the front into the auditorium where the audience sits. She was leaping like a gazelle up the aisle towards the back row of seats.

"Can you hear me now, Mum?"

"Yes! At last! Wherever are you?"

"I'm in the theatre."

"The theatre! What on earth are you doing there? I've been going out of my mind with worry."

"The door was open so I came in to have a look, and when I came out again you'd gone."

"Well I'm on my way now. Just stay put. And don't disturb anyone, all right?"

"All right."

Georgie pressed the red button to disconnect.

"What did she say?" Mitch called out to her from the stage.

"Stay put and don't disturb anyone," said Georgie.

Mitch laughed and quite a few of the others laughed too. Emma didn't though. She still looked furious. Georgie thought that the sooner Emma got her phone back the better. So she zipped to the front of the auditorium, and holding the phone in one hand, she used her free hand to help her spring up on to the stage in one quick movement.

"Thank you very much," she said in her politest voice as she handed the phone back to Emma.

Emma took it without a word. Then Georgie sprang back down again, sat in a front-row seat and tucked her legs up underneath her.

"I'll just sit here," she said to no one in particular. "I'll be as quiet as a little mouse until my mum gets here, I promise."

"Quiet as a little mouse, eh?" said a voice from close beside her. Georgie jumped. A few seats further along the row sat a big man with a beard and a leather jacket. He was chewing gum. Georgie didn't know if he'd been there all the time, but she didn't like to ask.

"What's your name, kid?"

"Georgie."

"Georgie, eh! You look like a dancer. Am I right?"

Georgie shook her head. "I don't have lessons or anything."

"But you like it. Right?"

"Right."

"Go back on the stage and show us a dance then, Georgie."

Emma stomped off, but the other actors didn't look at all cross. Georgie's body tingled all over as she got back up on the stage. She looked out at all the empty seats and went through her routine in her head. She'd done it millions of times in the playground because her friends at school were always getting her to show them how to do it. But she'd never ever danced on a real stage before, and her body was bursting with excitement as she began.

Georgie danced better than she'd ever danced in her life, and it was a shock to

24

hear the clapping at the end, because she'd been in her own little world.

"Good stuff!" said the important man, when the clapping stopped. "Come and sit next to me and watch the rehearsal now."

He leaned forwards, his elbows resting on his knees and his chin resting in his hands. Georgie saw out of the corner of her eye that he was watching the acting very carefully. She got herself into exactly the same position and pretended to be chewing too. This was turning out to be a really brilliant day!

Now that Georgie knew her mum was no longer missing, she felt completely happy just sitting there listening to the strange language. After a while she found she could understand quite a bit of it. It was like old-fashioned English.

About five minutes later an actor came

on to the stage wearing the huge donkey's head that Georgie had seen in the corridor. She couldn't help giggling. And when Emma started stroking and kissing the donkey's head, Georgie laughed out loud. This was such a funny play.

"OK, cut. Take five," the important man called out.

Immediately everyone stopped acting and left the stage. Georgie bit her lip. The man was obviously so cross about Georgie laughing that he'd stopped the rehearsal. Any second now he would probably give her a big telling-off. Georgie held her breath and closed her eyes.

★ ★ ★

Chapter Five

"Your mum's here, Georgie."

It was Mitch's voice, and when she looked up she saw that he was holding the donkey's head.

"Was that *you* in there, Mitch?"

"Certainly was!"

Then her mum came running down the steps at the side of the stage.

"Georgie, come on! Right this minute. You're not allowed in here."

"That's all right," said the important

man, sticking his hand out to shake hands with Georgie's mum. "My name's Tim."

"Pleased to meet you," said Georgie's mum. "And I'm so sorry about my daughter. I'll get her out from under your feet now, and then you can carry on in peace."

Georgie felt a terrible sadness coming over her. It had been magical watching the rehearsal and doing her routine on the stage. She hated the thought of having to leave. Her mum had already turned to go.

"Can I come again tomorrow?" she blurted out to Mitch.

"Not up to me," said Mitch, looking at Tim.

"Sure you can," said Tim.

"Oh thank you," said Georgie. "Thank you very, very much."

She felt like dancing round the whole theatre because it looked as though Tim wasn't cross, after all.

"Want to see the donkey's head before you go?" Mitch asked.

"Yeah!" said Georgie as she took a run at the stage and leapt up in one bound.

"Impressive!" said Tim. Then he turned to Georgie's mum. "Is she always as bouncy and quick-flash as this?"

Georgie's mum pursed her lips and nodded.

"Pity we can't use her in the play," Tim said with a thoughtful look in his eyes.

"What about Chickweed?" Mitch asked Tim.

"Come on now, Georgie," said her mum, who had gone up the steps at

the side of the stage and was waiting in the wings.

Out of the corner of her eye Georgie could see that her mum had her hands on her hips, and was wearing her mega-impatient look.

Georgie kept stroking the donkey's furry head. She was praying that Tim and Mitch would say something else about her being in the play, instead of talking about chickweed, whatever that was.

"Come on, Georgie, hurry up!" hissed her mum.

"You'd better go," Mitch said quietly.

"Bye Mitch," said Georgie, leaving the stage sadly.

"Seeya," he replied, patting her head.

"Don't ever do anything like that again," said her mum, as soon as they were out of the theatre. "I had absolutely no idea where you were."

"But at least I phoned you... That was sensible, wasn't it?" Georgie said, trying to get her mum in a good mood.

"You shouldn't have needed to phone me in the first place, young lady." And her mum's hand gripped Georgie's tightly as she marched briskly along.

"I'm very sorry," Georgie said quickly because she didn't want this to turn into a great big telling-off. "It was so brilliant though. You *will* let me go back to watch again tomorrow, won't you? Tim said it was OK, didn't he?"

"He was just being polite. The last thing he needs is a little girl getting in the way."

"But I didn't get in the way. I stayed perfectly still and quiet."

Georgie bit her lip because she knew that wasn't quite true.

"Well I could see at least one person on the stage who didn't look too pleased," said her mum.

"That was Emma. I borrowed the phone from her."

"Well no wonder she wasn't looking pleased! You must have caused a terrible kerfuffle. I'm sorry, Georgie, but I'm not letting you go back."

"But Tim said it was a shame they couldn't use me in the play."

"Well, there you are, you see. *It's a shame* they can't, but they can't. And that's the end of that. So let's get to the library before it shuts."

Chapter Six

After tea, Georgie watched telly with her big brothers, Damian, who was fifteen, and Aaron, who was thirteen. They knew that their mum was cross with Georgie, and they wanted all the details.

"So when you crept in through that door, Georgie, did anyone see you?" asked Aaron.

"One of the actors saw me because I made a noise, by mistake."

"What was the name of the play?" asked Damian.

Georgie screwed up her face and stared at the ceiling, trying to remember if anyone had actually said the name of the play.

"Well, what was it about?" Damian asked her, a bit impatiently. "We might have done it at school."

"It was difficult to understand because they all spoke in funny old-fashioned English."

"Sounds like a Shakespeare play," said Damian.

"There was a donkey's head in it," Georgie told him.

"It must be *A Midsummer Night's Dream* then."

Georgie clapped her hands together and said, "Yesss!"

She had no idea if Damian was right or not, but that didn't matter.

"A lady was stroking the donkey's head," she explained, feeling very important.

"She must have been playing the part of Titania," said Damian. "That's the Queen of the Fairies."

"The Queen of the Fairies!" breathed Georgie. "So when they do the play with the audience watching, Titania will be wearing a floaty fairy costume, I expect."

She closed her eyes to imagine Emma all dressed up as a Fairy Queen. When she opened them again she saw that her brothers had moved closer to the television. They must have got bored with talking about the play.

"And what are all the other fairies

called?" asked Georgie, trying to get the conversation going again.

"Ssh!" said Aaron.

"Just tell me their names, then I'll shush," said Georgie.

"There's a book about it in the bookcase somewhere," said Damian, moving even closer to the telly.

Georgie rushed over to the bookcase and read all the titles until she came to *A Midsummer Night's Dream.*

"Brilliant!"

She sat cross-legged on the floor, turning the pages slowly because there were lots of pictures.

Spread right across the middle pages of the book was the most beautiful picture of all the fairies, with Titania in the middle.

Underneath the picture of each fairy

was the fairy's name. Georgie read each name out loud. Her brothers weren't too pleased.

"Peaseblossom…"

"Ssh!"

"Cobweb…Moth…"

"Shush!"

"Mustardseed…"

"Be quiet!"

Georgie whispered the last one.

"Chickweed…" Then her eyes opened wide and she shouted at the top of her voice, "Chickweed!"

"Shut up, Georgie!"

But Georgie was too excited to shut up. She ran into the kitchen bursting with her big discovery. "Mum! Mitch thinks I could be one of the fairies!"

★ ★ ★

Chapter Seven

"What *are* you talking about, Georgie?"

"Well, you know Mitch said to Tim, 'What about Chickweed?' Well, I've just found out that Chickweed is one of the fairies in the play."

Georgie's eyes were shining. Her fists were clenched together under her chin. "Please let me go back there tomorrow, Mum. It would be the best thing ever if I could act on a proper stage with real actors in front of an audience."

Georgie's mum looked serious.

"Mitch is just one of the actors, Georgie. Tim is the man in charge. He's the director of the play. I'm sure if he'd wanted you as a fairy, he would have said so when Mitch suggested it, wouldn't he?"

Georgie scowled. It was true that Tim hadn't replied when Mitch had said the word "Chickweed". Maybe her mum was right, and he was just being kind to her because she was a little girl.

"But can't I just go anyway. Oh please, Mum. Pleeeeease."

"Well *I* can't take you — I'm at work tomorrow," said her mum.

"Aaron and Damian can take me. They won't mind," said Georgie. Georgie's mum frowned at the cooker. "Please, Mum. You'll be my best friend..."

"Don't talk such nonsense. I know you're desperate to go, but I just don't think it would be right."

"Oh Mum! Why not?"

"Firstly because you weren't invited. You invited *yourself*..."

"But how could Tim know that I wanted to come back if I didn't ask if I was allowed?"

"Don't interrupt. Secondly, Aaron and Damian haven't been invited..."

"They could drop me off and come back later and collect me... Oh please, Mum?"

Georgie's mum was looking crosser and crosser. "Stop whining, Georgie! If you stay on your own, Tim will feel as though he ought to keep an eye on you. And he can't be thinking about little girls when he's trying to direct a play..."

"Oh Mum, pleeeeease!"

"The answer is no! End of conversation!"

Chapter Eight

At half past nine the following morning Georgie was talking to her friend Jessica on the phone. Georgie told Jessica why she was so fed up and Jessica thought of two brilliant plans – plan A and plan B.

"Good luck!" she said to Georgie.

When Georgie put the phone down she went out into the garden, her heart beating fast. Her brothers were weeding the big flower bed at the back. They were working hard, because the more they got done, the more pocket money they got.

Georgie took a deep breath, but tried to hide it.

"You know how I went into the theatre and watched the actors yesterday?" she began.

"You're not going there today 'cos Mum says you can't," Damian told her quickly.

So that was the end of plan A. Now for plan B. But it was important to wait at least ten minutes, otherwise her brothers would guess what she was up to. So she sat on the back doorstep and told them a funny story that she'd read in her magazine.

When she guessed that ten minutes was up, Georgie said, "What day is it?"

"Tuesday."

"I thought so. My new magazine never came this morning."

No answer.

"Can we go down to the paper shop and collect it? I'm bored."

Damian stopped weeding. "Yeah, let's have a break."

Aaron just nodded and chucked his trowel on the soil.

Georgie's stomach was doing excited back flips as the three of them set off to the paper shop.

"I'm going to do my routine to that tree and back," she said.

The boys were taking turns to kick a stone, which kept on going into the hedge. Neither of them was really paying attention to Georgie. When she got to the tree, she looked back and saw

44

that they were laughing and pushing each other out of the way, both trying to kick the stone.

Right, thought Georgie. This is it! She ran like the wind as hard as she could, never turning round. But after a minute she could hear her brothers shouting.

"Oi! Georgie! Come back here!"

Georgie knew they'd start running to catch up with her at any second. Her heart was beating even faster, partly because of the running, partly because of the adventure and partly because of the naughtiness.

As she got nearer the theatre she prayed that the door would be open. It was. Not daring to look behind she just plunged inside and pulled it gently shut.

Immediately she could hear the voices of the actors on the stage. She was

expecting someone to turn round at any second and say, *Will you turn that loud heartbeat down! I can't hear myself think with all that racket!*

But no one spoke, so Georgie tiptoed round the corner and saw Emma and four other ladies on the side of the stage.

Uh-oh!

Somehow she had to get into the auditorium before her brothers showed up. They'd never dare go past the actors.

Georgie screwed up all her courage and went up to Emma and the others. Not one of them even noticed that she was right behind them, they were watching the stage so carefully. But Georgie didn't think she should tap anyone on the back in case they jumped, like Mitch had done yesterday.

Maybe it would be possible to crawl

46

round the actors' legs. Georgie crouched down. And that was when she realised she wasn't the only girl in the theatre. Sitting in the very middle of the audience's seats, eating a chocolate bar, was a girl who looked about Georgie's age. She was staring at the floor as she chewed the chocolate. She looked really bored. When she caught sight of Georgie, her eyes lit up and she beckoned with her hand.

Georgie did a thumbs up sign, then darted round the adults' legs, trying not to touch anyone. Then she raced down the steps and slipped into the seat next to the girl.

"Hi, I'm Georgie," she whispered. "Who are you?"

The girl didn't answer that question, but she looked really pleased to see

Georgie. "My dad told me about you. He said you might come today," she whispered excitedly. Then she called out in a voice that rang all round the theatre, "Dad, Georgie's here!"

Everyone stopped what they were doing on the stage and Tim turned round from the front row. Georgie gasped. The girl was Tim's daughter.

"Hey, Georgie, you made it! Terrific!"

Georgie gave him her best smile. Everything was so different from yesterday. It didn't seem to matter about talking loudly and interrupting the play today.

Tim leaned forwards and looked suddenly serious. "How d'you fancy being one of the fairies in the play, Georgie?"

Georgie couldn't speak she was so

happy. She just nodded hard and kept smiling.

"Are *you* going to be one of the fairies too?" she asked the girl beside her.

The girl shook her head hard. "No way!"

"Megan's just watching," said Tim. "She's been dying for you to arrive..."

Megan scowled and sighed a huge sigh as her father went all serious again. "OK, here's what you have to do..."

Then Tim explained exactly where Georgie should run – or "fly" as he called it. "Up on tiptoes. Fairy footsteps, light as a feather."

So Georgie went up the steps into the wings and kicked off her trainers and socks. Most of the actresses were smiling at her. But Emma wasn't. She looked cross about being interrupted again.

"Your name's Chickweed," whispered one of the ladies. "You're the little baby fairy. Emma's the Queen of the Fairies."

Georgie turned to Emma. "I know…you're Titania!" she said.

Emma looked surprised.

"She's done her homework!" said one of the other ladies, winking at Georgie.

Surely Emma will smile now! thought Georgie. But she didn't. "Get ready for your music," was all she said.

Georgie didn't need telling twice. She stretched out her arms, and stood on her highest tiptoes ready to whizz across the stage. But then a cold shiver ran down her spine when someone spoke right behind her.

"What d'you think you're doing?"

"She's doing as she's told," Emma hissed. "Who are *you*, anyway?"

"Her brother — and she's not allowed in the theatre."

A murmur went through all the grown-ups at the side of the stage. Georgie came down from her tiptoes. But then she heard her music starting and rose back up again. She closed her eyes to block out the talking around her, and pretended she was Chickweed zooming down from a glittering sky.

Round the stage and down the steps, she ran, lighter and faster than she'd ever run before. Right to the back of the auditorium then down the side and back on to the stage. She felt as though she really *was* flying. It was totally wicked!

"That's brilliant!" called Tim as she whirled round on the stage, then settled in the corner at the front just as he'd told her.

The rest of the actors clapped and smiled.

"Cool!" called a clear voice from the auditorium. And when Georgie looked up she saw that Megan was giving her the thumbs up.

"Is your mum around, boys?" Tim asked Aaron and Damian.

"She's at work," said Damian. "She'll be back at half past two."

"She said Georgie wasn't allowed to come here today," Aaron added.

"Ah!" said Tim. And in that one little sound Georgie felt as though her brilliant dream was over. Tim closed his eyes and stared at the ceiling for a few seconds. When he looked back he sounded very brisk. "I'll give her a ring later, Georgie and see what she says. If it's a yes, you get to be the fairy, Chickweed, in the play. But if she says no…" He shrugged. "…we'll just have to manage without you."

For a moment Georgie's heart felt as though it had moved up to her mouth. But then she didn't have time to think about anything except being Chickweed, learning when it was her turn to pretend to fly, and remembering exactly where she had to go.

She thought she'd never concentrated so hard in her whole life.

"Well done," said Tim, after what seemed like ages and ages. "You can go whenever you want. I'll phone your mum later."

Georgie went to say bye to Megan,

but when she looked over to where Megan had been sitting, the seat was empty.

Chapter Nine

Georgie made her brothers promise not to breathe a single word of what had happened that day to their mum.

"Let's wait till Tim phones and explains it all," she said. "Mum won't be able to say no to Tim, will she?"

"Huh! Don't you believe it!" said Damian. "Once she realises you've disobeyed her, she'll go ballistic! You ought to say sorry first."

"What's ballistic?"

"You'll soon find out. She's just walked past this window. I'm out of here!" said Aaron.

"Me too," Damian agreed.

"Hi Mum!" they called, as they scooted upstairs. "Did you see the garden?"

Their mum was coming through the back door into the kitchen. "Yes, I did, and I'm impressed... Whatever's the matter, Georgie? You don't look at all well."

Georgie gulped and took a deep breath.

"I...I...I'm very sorry because I know you said I wasn't allowed..."

The worried look on her mum's face changed in a flash.

"You haven't been back to that theatre, have you?"

She looked ready to explode. Georgie started explaining at top speed.

"You see Tim said I could be in the play. He really wanted me to be the baby fairy. I only popped in to peep, but he asked me to stay and to pretend to fly…"

"Aaron! Damian!" called Georgie's mum. "Come down here. What exactly happened today, boys?"

So Georgie's mum heard the whole story of how Georgie tricked the boys and went into the theatre. She was furious.

"I think we'd better get down to the Playhouse and have a word with Tim," she said, grabbing Georgie's hand.

Afternoon rehearsal was in full swing. Georgie and her mum stood in the wings. Mitch saw them there from the stage and signalled to Tim.

"Ah!" smiled Tim. "I was going to phone you, Mrs…"

"Rivers," came the crisp reply.

Georgie followed her mum down the steps and over to where Tim was standing in the front row.

"I'd like to offer Georgie a part in the play," said Tim.

Georgie's whole body tingled when she heard those words. But her mum's face looked just as stern as ever.

"If Georgie hadn't disobeyed me, I might have considered it. But under the circumstances I'm afraid the answer is no."

Georgie looked down. She felt like crying, except that she never cried.

Tim shrugged. "That's a shame. She's a very talented young lady, and the

play would be all the better for having her in it."

"Well, I'm sorry…"

"Pleeeeease, Mum."

"The answer is no."

Then everyone turned at the sound of the bright clear voice coming from the middle of the auditorium.

"Georgie's really great. You ought to watch her – just once."

Megan was patting the seat beside her, as though she was saving it for her best friend. "Come on."

Georgie's mum was too surprised to speak. She just walked to Megan's row, looking as though she was in a dream, and sat down beside her.

Tim didn't waste a second. "Places," he said.

Everyone got ready in a flash. Georgie

dashed up to the side, rose on to her tiptoes and closed her eyes.

As soon as the music started she forgot everything except her part. She whirled and whizzed through the shimmering sky and over the feathery tops of the glistening trees, until she came to rest in the flowery garden with Titania.

There was a long silence when the music stopped. Georgie looked at her mum. She was sitting perfectly still and staring straight ahead. Everyone was watching her, waiting to hear what she would say.

"She's good, isn't she?" Tim said.

"No," said Mrs Rivers, turning slowly to face him. "She's bad!" Then she got up and walked towards the stage. Georgie stood up, knees trembling, waiting to hear what her mum would say next. "You *were* bad..." Her mum's mouth was beginning to turn up at the corners. "But OK, I admit it – you were also pretty good!"

Georgie jumped down from the stage and hugged her mum tightly. Then, as all the grown-ups started talking and laughing amongst themselves, she rushed over to Megan.

"You were very brave to talk to my mum like that," whispered Georgie. She's really strict."

"I'm used to strict people," said Megan. And she looked so fed up and sad that Georgie felt sorry for her. "I'll ask Mum if you can come to tea," she said.

Megan's eyes sparkled. "Cool!"

"Right, let's get back to work," Tim called out.

Georgie shot to her place and stood with her toe pointed, ready for her music.

"I didn't think you could do it," said a voice behind her. "But I was wrong."

Georgie turned and got a shock because Emma was smiling at her. It was a lovely, warm smile, and Georgie felt as though she'd never been so happy in her life. Inside her head a new rap was bursting to get out...

"Well I'm gonna be a fairy
And I just can't wait
'Cos I'm in a proper play
And it feels so great!"